SURPRISE!

For Hannah

Thanks to David and Matt

Copyright © words & pictures 2017

First published in the UK in 2017

by words & pictures, an imprint of Quarto Publishing Plc,

The Old Brewery, 6 Blundell Street, London N7 9BH

British Library Cataloguing in Publication Data available on request

ISBN 978 191027 736 2

1 3 5 7 9 8 6 4 2

Printed in China

SURPRISE!

Mike Henson

words & pictures

"SSSShh!"

"Huh?"

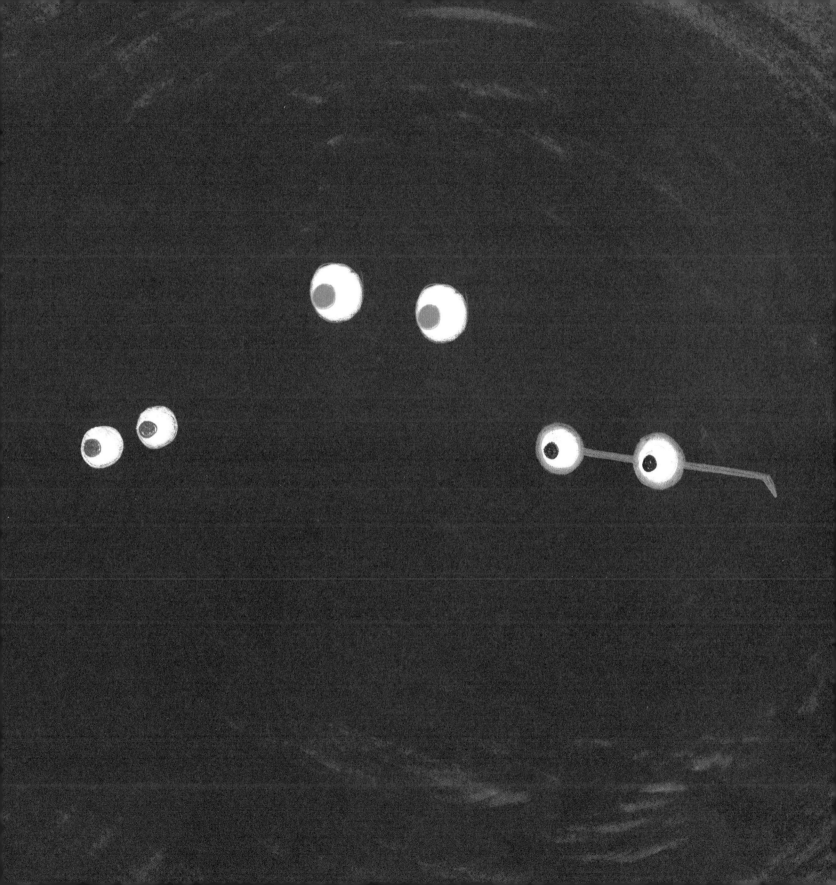

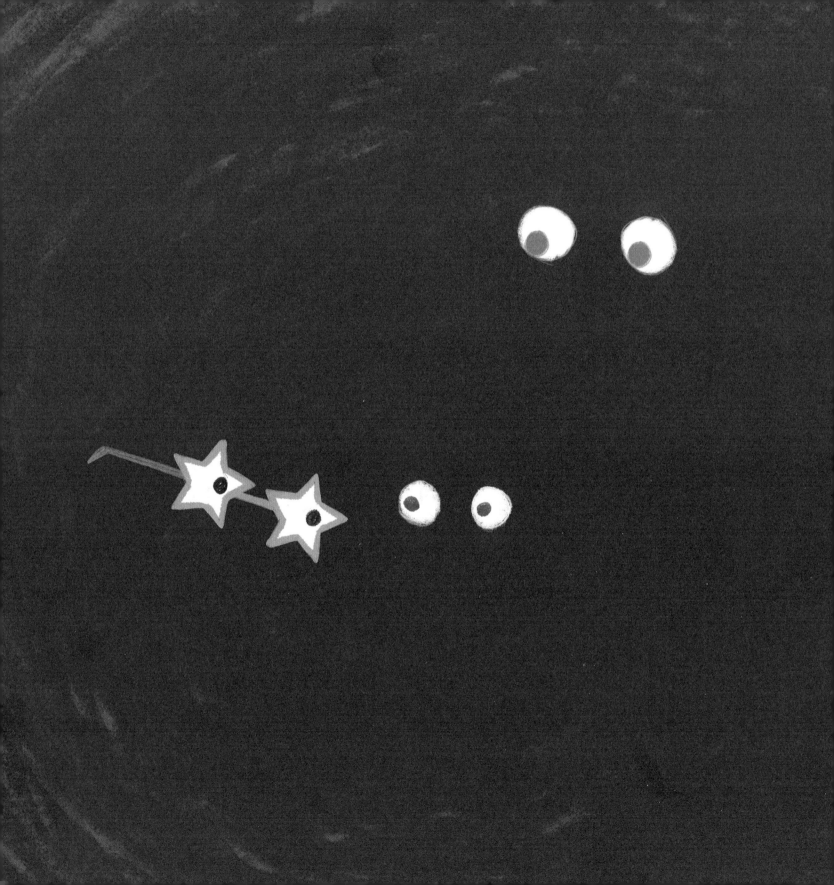

"Surprise!"

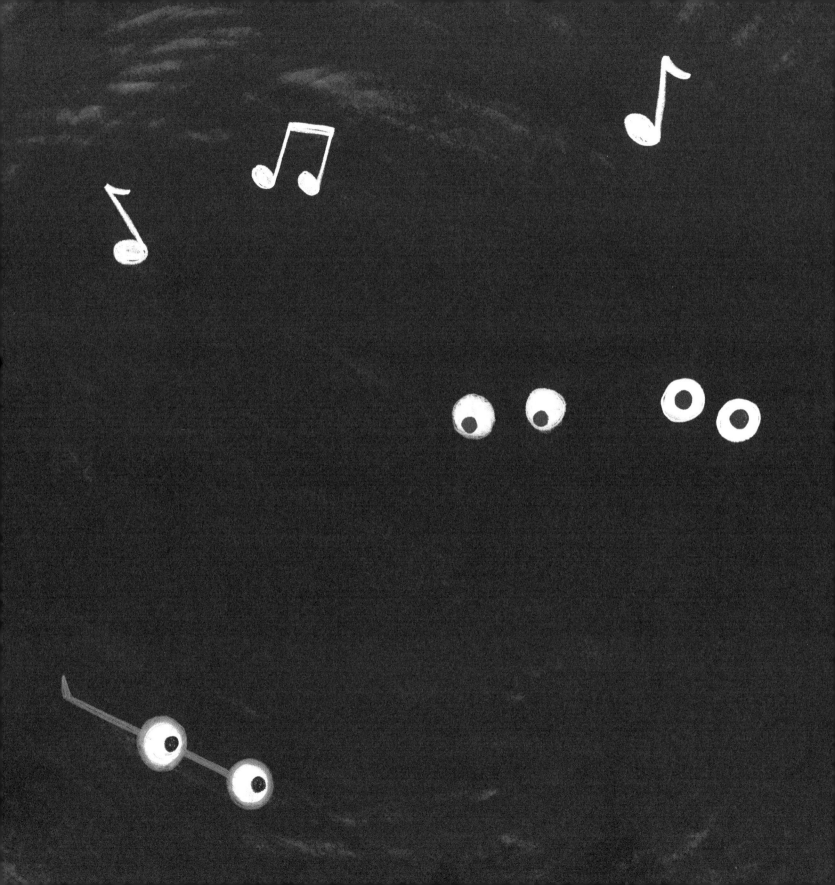

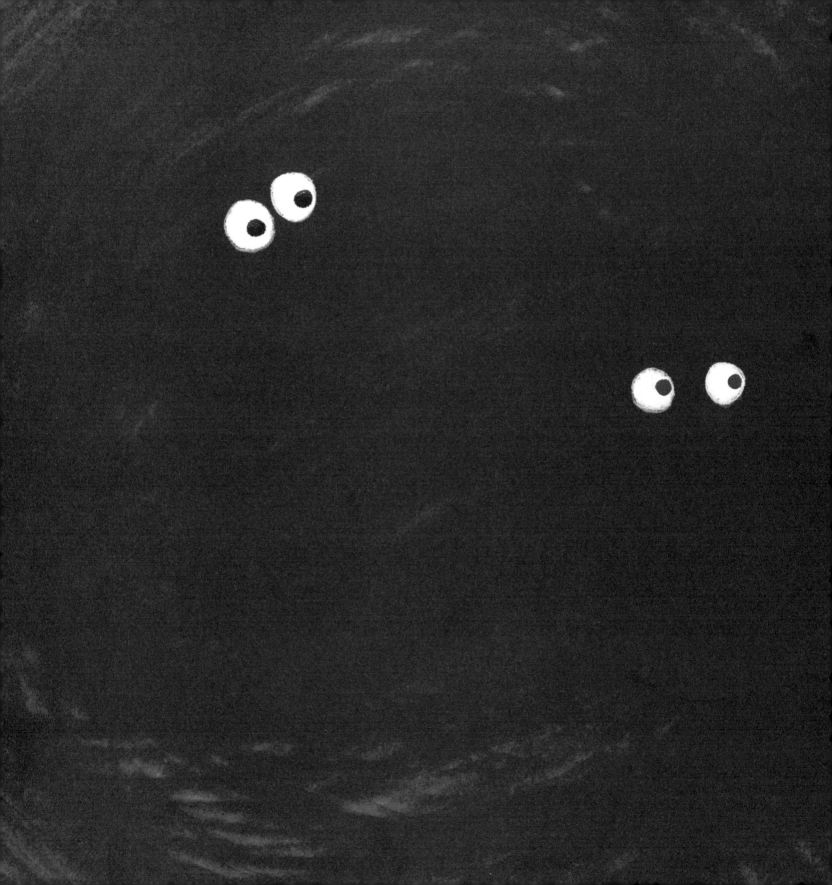

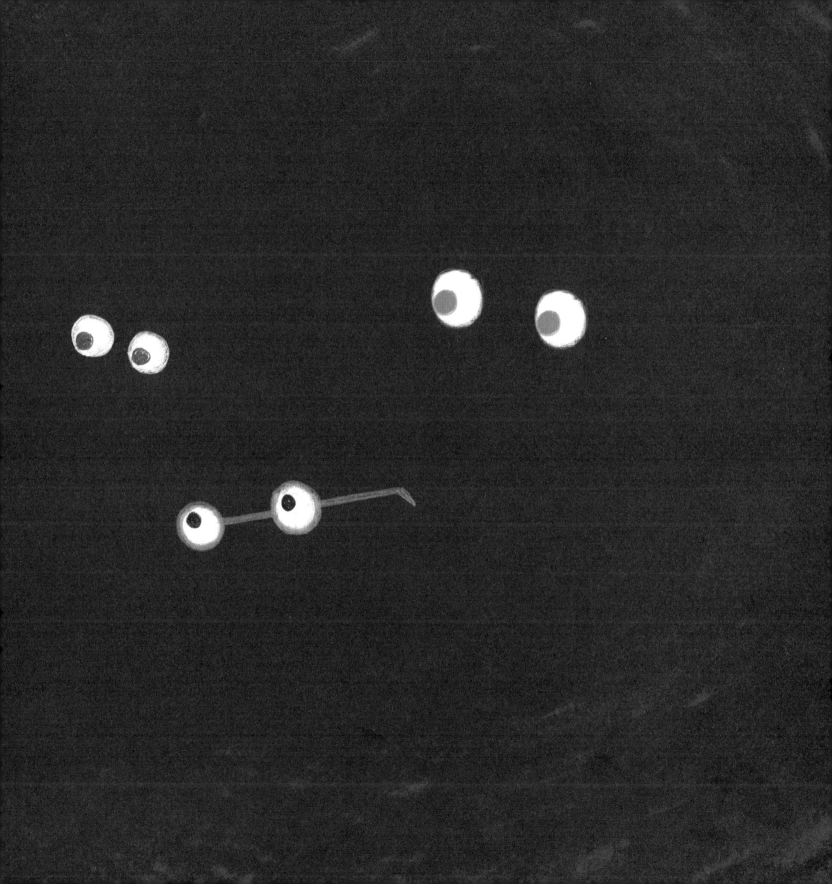

"Oh my!
This party
is amazing!...

...Every time
the light goes on,
there's a fantastic..."

"Huh?"

"Oooh!"